P9-DXK-676

Some of the oldest drawings ever found were made more than thirty thousand years ago in a cave in southern France. In that same cave is the footprint of an eight-year-old child. Alongside it, the footprint of a wolf.

For Susan, with love.
Your beautiful drawings
open our eyes to
our own imaginations.

—MG

Little, Brown and Company • Hachette Book Group • 237 Park Avenue, New York, NY 10017
Visit our website at www.lb-kids.com • Little, Brown and Company is a division of Hachette Book Group, Inc.

First Edition: September 2013 • Library of Congress Cataloging-in-Publication Data
Gerstein, Mordicai, author, illustrator. • The first drawing / by Caldecott Medalist Mordicai Gerstein. — First edition.
pages cm • Summary: Thirty thousand years ago, an imaginative child sees the shapes of animals in clouds and on the walls of the cave he shares with his family, but no one else can see them until he makes the world's first drawing. Includes author's note on cave drawings. • ISBN 978-0-316-20478-1 • [1. Drawing—Fiction. 2. Imagination—Fiction. 3. Cave dwellers—Fiction. 4. Prehistoric peoples—Fiction. 5. Cave paintings—Fiction.] I. Title.
PZ7.G325Fir 2013 • [E]—dc23 • 2013001269
10 9 8 7 6 5 4 3 2 • SC • Printed in China

MORDICAI GERSTEIN

THE FIRST DRAWING

LITTLE, BROWN AND COMPANY
NEW YORK BOSTON

Imagine...

you were born before the invention of drawing,
more than thirty thousand years ago.

You live in a cave with your parents, grandparents, sisters, brothers, uncles, aunts, many cousins, and your wolf, Shadow. It's a big cave.

You love to watch animals.
You see them everywhere.
You see them at the river where they come
to drink: horses, giant elk, reindeer,
woolly rhinoceroses, bears, sometimes lions, and more.
You sit and watch them for hours.

You see the grand white and gray clouds
that drift over the valley.
Their ever-changing shapes look to you
like a parade of animals.
“Papa! That cloud looks like
a woolly mammoth.”
“It looks to me,” says your father, “like a cloud.”

When collecting stones for spearheads and knives,
you think some look like animals, too.
"Mama! This stone looks like a bear!"
"To me," says your mother, "it looks like a stone."
You wonder, *Why can't they see what I see?*

At night, wrapped in deerskins, you see shadow images of all the animals again in the firelight flickering over the bumps and hollows of the cave walls. And they seem to move.

"Look, Mama—galloping horses!"

"What horses? Go to sleep."

"Papa, Grandpa, there on the ceiling—elk!"

"There are no elk. Go to sleep!"
"Sisters, brothers, cousins,
don't you see the rhinoceroses?"
"No!" shouts everyone.
"Now go to sleep!"

They call you “Child Who Sees What Isn’t There.”
How can you make them see what you see?
Every night you watch the animals on the walls.
Then you dream you’re running with them, like one of them.

One morning you're out with your father searching for stones. You wander off around a hill of huge boulders.

You look up
and see, right in front of you...

...a **WOOLLY MAMMOTH**!

It's not made of lights and shadows or clouds.

You can smell it, warm and musky.

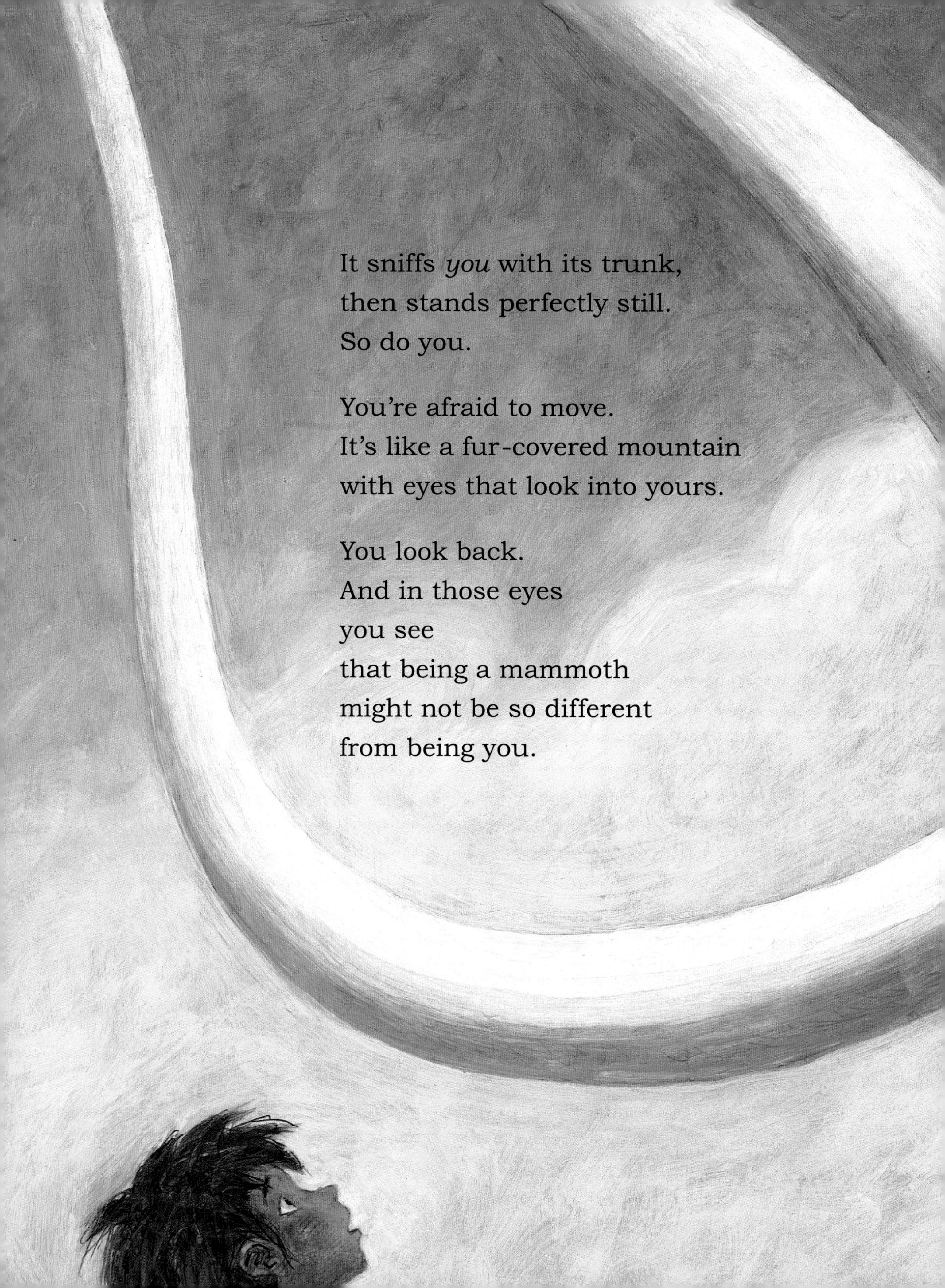

It sniffs *you* with its trunk,
then stands perfectly still.
So do you.

You're afraid to move.
It's like a fur-covered mountain
with eyes that look into yours.

You look back.
And in those eyes
you see
that being a mammoth
might not be so different
from being you.

The mammoth sighs through its trunk.
And like a mountain walking,
it turns and slowly lumbers away.
You begin to breathe again.

“Papa, right in front of me!
A woolly—”

"Child! Child!" Your father sighs.
"What are we going to
do with you?"

That night, in front of the fire,
as your eyes begin to close,
you see...

...an image on the wall, so big and so real.
You sit up and say,
“Yow!”

"Huh?" says your father.

"What's wrong?" says your mother.

"Look...on the wall!
It looks like it's **breathing**!"
"There's nothing," they say. "Go to sleep."
"But **look**—the tail, the tusks...
why don't you see it?"

Now everyone is awake.

“There’s nothing to see.

Go to sleep!”

“How can I make you **see**...?”

And without thinking, you leap out of bed,
take a burnt stick from the fire, and run to the wall.

"Look! Here's the tail. Here, the back legs."
You make marks on the bumpy wall to show them where to look.

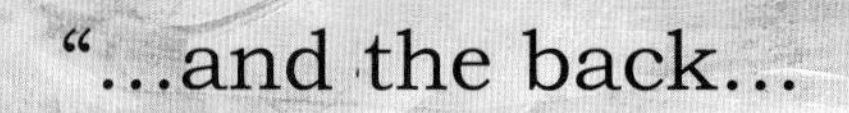

"...and the back...

the front legs...

“the ears...the eye—watching us...its trunk...and its tusks—”

“STOP!” shouts your father.

He aims his spear at the wall.
Everyone huddles by the doorway,
the wide-eyed children clutching
their parents' legs.
"I can see it!" gasps your father.
"This...is **MAGIC**!"

"No, Papa," you say. "I'm just showing you...."

And you look at what you've done.
You have made the world's first drawing.

"Yes!" you say.
"It ***is* magic**!"

Now everyone can see what you see.
And so you make more drawings.

You show your parents,
grandparents, sisters,
brothers, uncles, aunts,
and cousins how to draw, too.

For thousands of years,
people keep drawing.

Even today, people are still doing it.
And that's how—
if you'd been around
more than thirty thousand years ago—
you might have invented drawing.

And it's *still* **magic**!

Author's Note

In 1994, a cave was discovered in southern France. On its walls were drawings made more than thirty thousand years ago, fifteen thousand years older than all the other drawings known at the time.

Instead of being simpler and cruder, as would be expected, this newly discovered work was, if anything, more beautiful and elegant than what was done later. In the same cave, a human footprint was found—that of an eight-year-old child.

Of course, no one knows exactly who made the world's first drawing, or how it happened. And there are new discoveries being made all the time of drawings that might be even older than those found in this cave. But for someone who has drawn all his life, it has always seemed obvious that whoever invented drawing must have been a child. It's hard to imagine children not drawing. But how many adults do you know who draw? When I read of the child's footprint in the cave, I said to myself, "Aha! I was right!"

This story is my imagined version of how and why drawing was invented. Drawing is the method we have to show others what we see and how we feel about what we see. It is a way to explore and share the vast, invisible world of our imaginations.

And to me, *that* is magic.

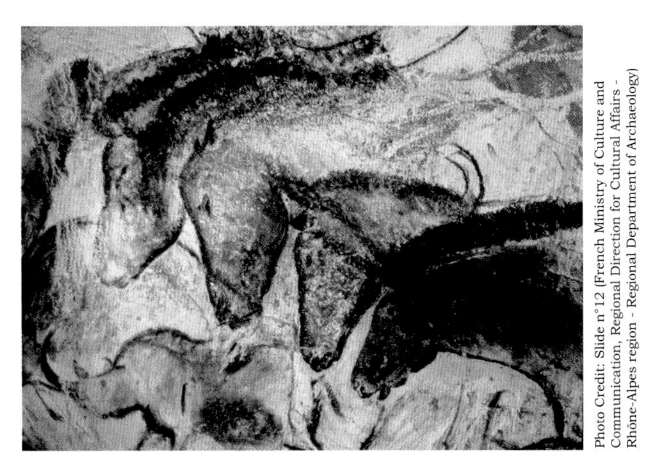

Photo Credit: Slide n°12 (French Ministry of Culture and Communication, Regional Direction for Cultural Affairs - Rhône-Alpes region - Regional Department of Archaeology)

Pictured here are horses and a rhinoceros from the Chauvet-Pont-d'Arc cave in southern France, the inspiration for the cave in this book.

About This Book

The illustrations for this book were done in acrylics, pen and ink, and colored pencil on Strathmore 2-ply plate finish paper.
The text was set in Bookman Old Style, and the display type is Lithos Pro.
This book was edited by Alvina Ling and designed by Patti Ann Harris. The production was supervised by Jonathan Lopes, and the production editor was Wendy Dopkin.